To Addy

From Mom & Dad

We may have put the book and illustrations together but make no mistake; this is YOUR STORY!

We are so proud of you and your creative mind.

Never stop writing!

Special thanks to Mrs. Henderson. You have inspired Addison and have seen the wonder in her imagination. You have made a lasting impact.

First Edition published by Temple Knight Publishing, 2024
Copyright © Addison Rosemary Schloesser, 2024

Written by Addison Rosemary Schloesser
Illustrations copyright © 2024 by Nathan Schloesser
Book design by Nathan & Jennifer Schloesser
Editing & proof reading by Jennifer Schloesser
Contributions by Landon, Emmalyn, Bailee, & Brynlee Schloesser

Scarecrow's Friends

A story about friendship & adventure.

Written by
Addison Rosemary

Temple Knight
PUBLISHING

One cold night
there was a
scarecrow.

He stood there
all night and day.

Through breakfast and
lunch and dinner until the
farmer fixed him up.

He found a crow.

She had a big beak.

It was black.

It was Halloween!

He thought "I am going to ask if I can be her friend."

He asked her and she said "Yes".

The crow stood on his shoulder.

They were friends forever.

They stood there with
their friends.

The animals stood together.

They were happy.

Everyone thought this was good.

But then it snowed.

Everyone was covered
with white snow.

Then it thawed out. The
sun was out. They all cheered.

Except for the crow and scarecrow
because that was not fun.

It was amazing.

They all jumped except
for the scarecrow because
he fell on his face.

The animals helped him up.

Then the crow flew off the tree.

He flew on the
scarecrow's shoulder.

Then they walked
to the sea.

They stood there,
the sea whooshed.

The scarecrow, the crow,
and the other animals
slipped and fell in the sea.

They were under a
boat and a shark.

Suddenly, they felt
a land of sand.

It was a farm.

The farmer said "You will be useful to scare the animals away."

When the farmer looked away, they ran away.

The farmer said "Oh no! Where is the scarecrow?"

The end.

Made in the USA
Columbia, SC
06 October 2024

43261498R00022